the MONSTER
at the end of this book

By Jon Stone

Illustrated by Michael Smollin

A GOLDEN BOOK • NEW YORK

Golden Books, A Golden Book, and the G colophon are registered trademarks of Penguin Random House LLC.
randomhousekids.com   SesameStreetBooks.com   www.sesamestreet.org
Educators and librarians, for a variety of teaching tools, visit us at RHTeachersLibrarians.com
ISBN 978-0-375-97650-6
This special edition was printed for Kohl's Department Stores, Inc.
(for distribution on behalf of Kohl's Cares, LLC, its wholly owned subsidiary)
by Random House Children's Books, a division of Penguin Random House LLC, New York.

KOHL'S
Style: 97650
Factory Number: 126509
Production Date: 05/2017

MANUFACTURED IN CHINA
10 9 8 7 6 5 4 3 2 1
Random House Children's Books supports the First Amendment and celebrates the right to read.

This is a very dull page. What is on the next page?

Listen, I have an idea. If you do not turn **any pages**, we will never get to the end of this book.

And that is good, because there is a **Monster** at the end of this book.

So please do not turn the page.

Maybe you do not understand. You see, turning pages will bring us to the end of this book, and there is a **Monster** at the end of this book...

...but **this** will stop you from turning pages. See? I am tying the pages together so you cannot....

THERE! I, Grover, am nailing this page to the next one so that you will not be able to turn it, and we will not get any closer to the Monster at the end of this book.

ALL RIGHT!! ALL RIGHT! ALL RIGHT! ALL RIGHT!!

Do you know that every time you turn another page . . . you not only get us closer to the MONSTER at the end of this book, but you make a terrible mess!

The next page is the end of this book, and there is a **MONSTER** at the end of this book.

Oh, I am so **SCARED!**

Well, look at that! This is the end of the book, and the only one here is ...

ME

I, lovable, furry old GROVER, am the Monster at the end of this book.

And _you_ were so SCARED!

THE
END

I told you
and told you
there was
nothing to be
afraid of.